Copyright © 1998 by Nord-Süd Verlag AG, Gossau Zürich, Switzerland
First published in Switzerland under the title *Gustl Löwenmut*
English translation copyright © 1998 by North-South Books Inc.

All rights reserved.
No part of this book may be reproduced or utilized in any form
or by any means, electronic or mechanical, including photocopying,
recording, or any information storage and retrieval system,
without permission in writing from the publisher.

First published in the United States, Great Britain, Canada,
Australia, and New Zealand in 1998 by North-South Books,
an imprint of Nord-Süd Verlag AG, Gossau Zürich, Switzerland.

Library of Congress Cataloging-in-Publication Data is available.
A CIP catalogue record for this book is available from The British Library.
ISBN 1-55858-976-7 (trade binding)
1 3 5 7 9 TB 10 8 6 4 2
ISBN 1-55858-977-5 (library binding)
1 3 5 7 9 LB 10 8 6 4 2
Printed in Belgium

For more information about our books, and the authors and artists
who create them, visit our web site: http://www.northsouth.com

LUKE
THE LIONHEARTED

By Antonie Schneider

Illustrated by Cristina Kadmon

Translated by J. Alison James

NORTH–SOUTH BOOKS

New York ❖ London

When Luke woke up that first morning at Aunt Molly's,
he stretched with pleasure. He loved visiting his aunt.

Aunt Molly lived at the edge of town, with a big field and woods right behind her house. She was always cheerful and she let Luke do whatever he wanted.

He could bring worms into the house, or pop up at the
kitchen window, pretending to be a ghost, or climb trees, or
just sit quietly on the step and daydream.

That morning Aunt Molly asked Luke to deliver a loaf of
freshly baked bread to Peter Poole, who lived next door.
On the way across the field, Luke looked into the woods
and saw something that made him freeze with fear.

A lion, a real, live lion, lying right at the edge of the woods! Luke trembled all over. He squeezed his eyes shut. When he looked again, the lion had disappeared. Had he imagined it?

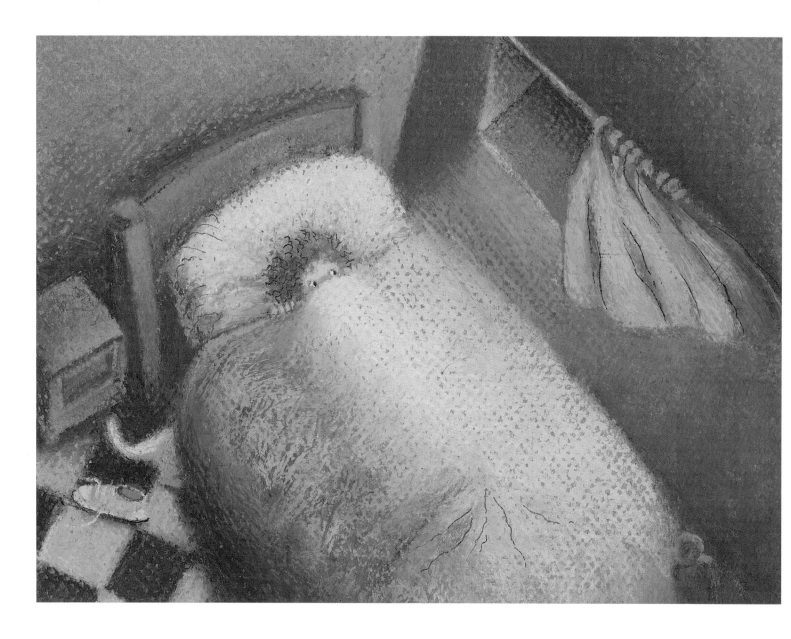

Luke ran into the house.

"What's the matter?" asked Aunt Molly.

"Nothing," said Luke.

All day long Luke stayed inside. And all day long he was afraid. Even when he was tucked safely into bed that night, he was still scared of the lion.

Luke started to cry.

"What's the matter?" asked Aunt Molly as she came into his room.

"I saw a lion at the edge of the woods," Luke said, sniffling.

Aunt Molly wrapped her arms around him and held him tightly. She was strong, Luke could tell, nearly as strong as a lion.

"Lions don't come into houses," Aunt Molly said. "Unless you invite them in."

Luke nodded. That made sense to him. Exhausted and relieved, he fell asleep in Aunt Molly's arms.

That night Luke dreamed of the lion. It stood outside the
garden gate, strong and tall, sniffing the sunflowers.
"Luke the Lionhearted!" roared the lion.

Luke heard his name quite clearly. Fearlessly he stepped outside, opened the garden gate, and said: "What do you want from me?"

The lion looked at him sadly and growled: "Help me, Luke the Lionhearted. I want to go home." With that, the lion disappeared.

When Luke woke up, he ran straight to the kitchen. "Aunt Molly," he said. "It was a real lion I saw yesterday."

Aunt Molly looked at Luke intently. "Are you sure?" she asked.

Just then there was an excited knocking on the door. It was Peter Poole, from next door. "Did you hear the news? There's a lion in our woods. It escaped from the zoo!"

Luke nodded at Aunt Molly and she nodded back.

Peter Poole said, "Anyone who sees him should tell the mayor at once."

Aunt Molly took Luke by the hand and they set off down the street to the town hall.

At the town hall Luke told how he'd seen the lion at the edge
of the woods. But he didn't say anything about his dream.
    He heard a siren, and the fire chief came in.
    "This is Luke," said the mayor. "He spotted the lion."

    Luke was thrilled to ride on the fire truck through the town.
The director of the zoo followed right behind.

When they got to the woods, a crowd had gathered. The zoo director asked Luke where he'd seen the lion, and the crowd watched in amazement as Luke fearlessly led the zoo director to the edge of the woods. "It was right here," said Luke.

The zoo director put a huge piece of meat on the grass.
"He will come," he said softly. "Are you afraid?"
Luke shook his head. He remembered his dream.

The lion did come. He looked bigger and stronger than Luke remembered. Bigger even than in the dream. Slowly he approached the meat.

Then Luke saw the zoo director press a tiny pipe to his lips,
and something flew through the air. It struck the lion.
The lion swayed and fell to the ground.

"Is he dead?" asked Luke, horrified.

"Come here," said the zoo director. "If you aren't afraid."

Luke approached the lion. It was strange, but he really wasn't frightened anymore. Maybe it had something to do with the dream.

"The lion is only asleep. You don't have to worry about him," said the zoo director. "But I have to get him safely back to the zoo before he wakes up. Many thanks, Luke. You have the heart of a lion!"

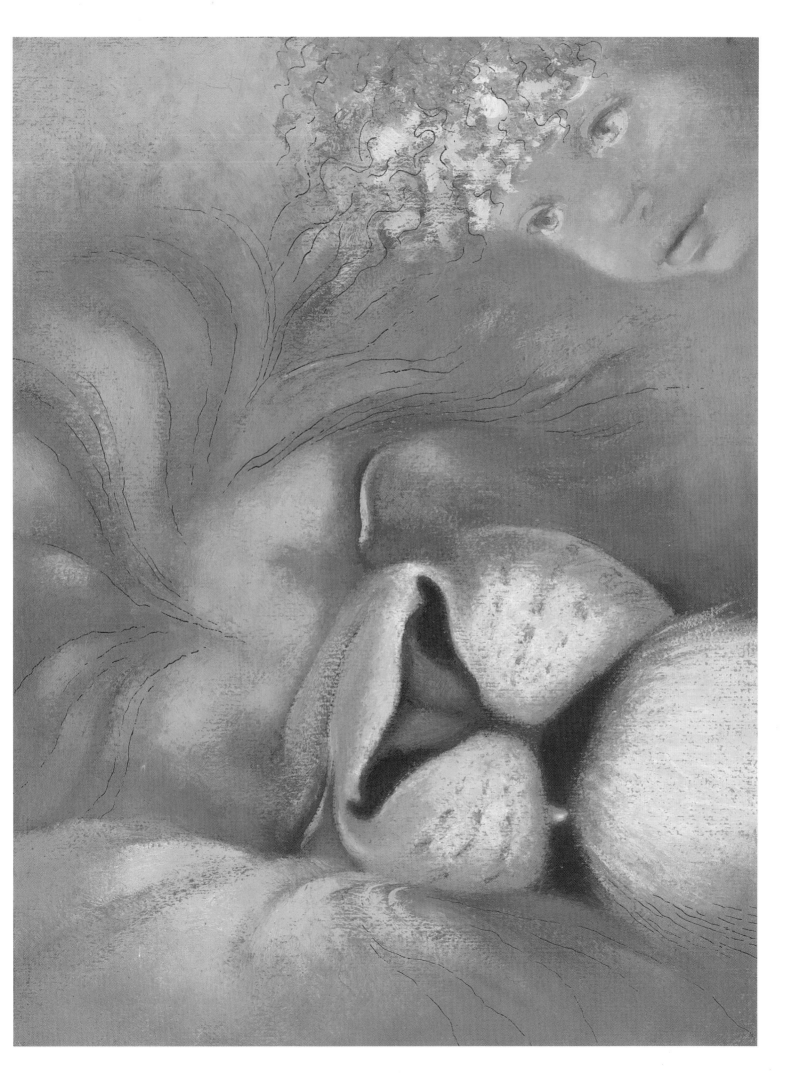

The crowd all watched as the lion was loaded into the zoo van.
Some of boys called out, "Luke the Lionhearted! Hooray for
Luke the Lionhearted!"

Luke grinned shyly and hurried back to Aunt Molly's house.

"Are you hungry?" asked Aunt Molly. "In all the excitement, you missed breakfast."

"I'm as hungry as a lion," said Luke, and he laughed.

That night in bed Luke thought of the things he would do tomorrow. Every day was fun at Aunt Molly's house—and sometimes very exciting, too.

Luke the Lionhearted was ready for anything.

$15.95

DATE			

NOV 2016